Goodnight Sammy

Written by Amanda C. Brown
Illustrated by Betsy Morningstar

Goodnight Sammy

FIRST SUNBURY PRESS EDITION

Printed in the United States of America

October 2011

ISBN 978-1-934597-82-8

Published by:

Sunbury Press, Inc.
2200 Market Street
Camp Hill, PA   17011

www.sunburypress.com

Camp Hill, Pennsylvania   USA

Sammy, my sweet little boy, inspired me to write this book.
Along our journey in creating this book, Betsy and I have
also found inspiration from our family and friends.
Thank you to all of those people who made it possible for
us to complete this journey.

--- Amanda C. Brown

In the Land of the Wubbies,
one special little wubbie
yearned for a friend.

He knew that all of the other wubbies in the land had already found friends.

"When would I find a friend?" asked
the lonely wubbie to the other wubbies.

While this lonesome
wubbie searched for
a friend, a little boy
named Sammy tossed
and turned in his crib.

Sammy had a hard time falling into a deep sleep at night.

Not even rocking on his favorite toy
would make him sleepy. Sometimes he'd
toss and turn and turn and toss in his
crib all night long.

Sammy's Mommy and Daddy would do everything they could to try to get Sammy to fall asleep. They would sing to him, rock him, and rub his back.

No matter what they tried, putting Sammy to sleep was not an easy thing to do.

One night, after Sammy's Mommy and Daddy sang songs and rubbed his back, Sammy finally drifted off to sleep.

But as Sammy slept, this night became unlike any other night.

Through the open window in Sammy's room, the lonely wubbie floated into the room. He landed on the rocking chair.

Sammy's dog listened quietly
as the wubbie began to sing.

As Sammy awoke, he was surprised to discover a wubbie singing a song on the rocking chair – right there in his room!

Sammy thought long and hard before
he knew what to say to wubbie.

Finally Sammy said, "What are you doing here?"

The wubbie quickly responded,
"I need a friend, and you need
help falling asleep."

Sammy's smile filled the room, and the lonely wubbie floated into Sammy's open arms and snuggled closely to Sammy.

"Ok, let's be friends. I think that I'll call you Walter," decided Sammy.

"Walter sounds like a perfect name for me. Thank you for being my friend," whispered the wubbie.

Within minutes,
Sammy and
Walter the wubbie
were fast asleep...

and Walter found the friend in Sammy
that he had always hoped for.

Amanda C. Brown (left) is a third grade teacher in central Pennsylvania where she lives with her devoted husband, Matt, and her adoring son, Sammy. Sammy's love for his very own wubbie was Amanda's inspiration for this series of children's books. She is excited to write more stories focusing on the fun and silly experiences that Sammy and the wubbies go through together as friends.

Betsy Morningstar (right) is an art teacher and artist who loves exploring art with children. She lives in Pennsylvania with her two hermit crabs, Ferdinand and Franco. She hopes young artists will be inspired to draw as they experience the connection between Sammy and Walter when reading this lovely bedtime story.